To Jake
With lots of love

Tabitha

Christmas 2001

TO AUDREY

FOR ALL THE FUN WE HAD

First published 1995 by Walker Books Ltd
87 Vauxhall Walk, London SE11 5HJ

2 4 6 8 10 9 7 5 3 1

This edition produced for
The Book People Ltd, Hall Wood Avenue,
Haydock, St Helens WA11 9UL

© 1995 Jill Murphy

This book has been typeset in Stone Informal.

Printed in Hong Kong

British Library Cataloguing in Publication Data
A catalogue record for this book is
available from the British Library.

ISBN 0-7445-3228-0

THE LAST
NOO-NOO

Jill Murphy

TED SMART

M arlon sat on the floor watching TV. Marlon's
granny sat in the armchair, watching Marlon.
"He's getting too old for that dummy," she said
sternly to Marlon's mum.
"It's a noo-noo," said Marlon.

"He calls it a noo-noo," explained Marlon's mum.
"Well, what*ever* he calls it," said Marlon's granny,
"he looks like an idiot with that stupid great *thing*
stuck in his mouth all the time."
"He doesn't have it *all* the time," soothed Marlon's
mum. "Only at night or if he's a bit tired.
He's a bit tired now – aren't you, pet?"
"Mmmmm," said Marlon.

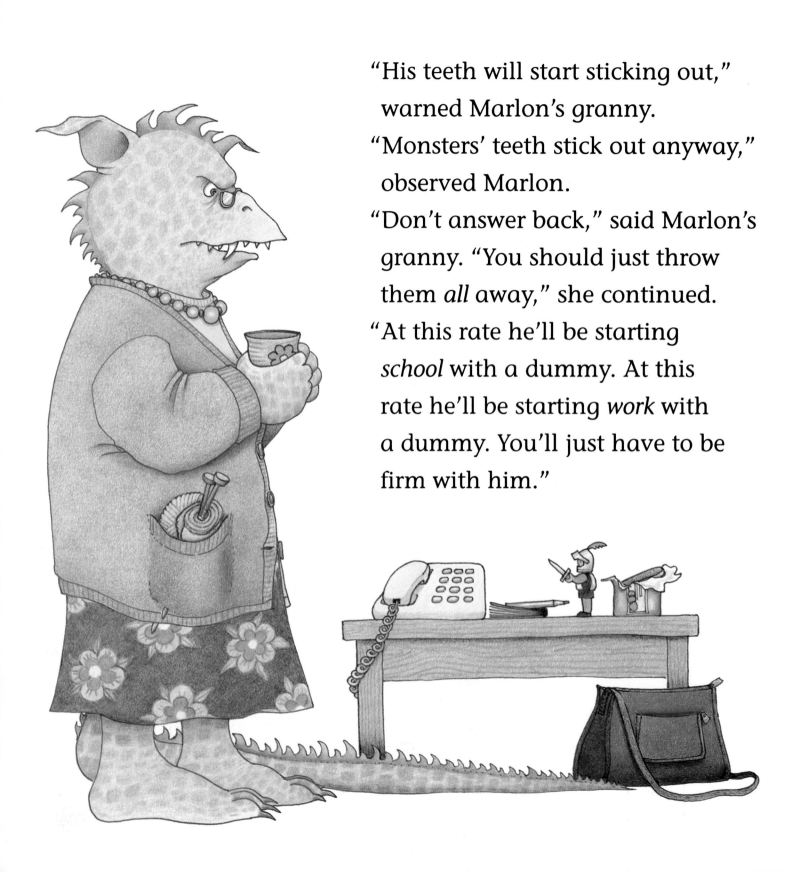

"His teeth will start sticking out," warned Marlon's granny. "Monsters' teeth stick out anyway," observed Marlon.

"Don't answer back," said Marlon's granny. "You should just throw them *all* away," she continued. "At this rate he'll be starting *school* with a dummy. At this rate he'll be starting *work* with a dummy. You'll just have to be firm with him."

"Well," said Marlon's mum, "I am *thinking* about it. We'll start next week, won't we Marlon? Now you're a big boy, we'll just get rid of all those silly noo-noos, won't we?"

"No," said Marlon.

"You see!" said Marlon's granny. "One word from you and he does as he likes."

There was no doubt about it. Marlon was a hopeless case.

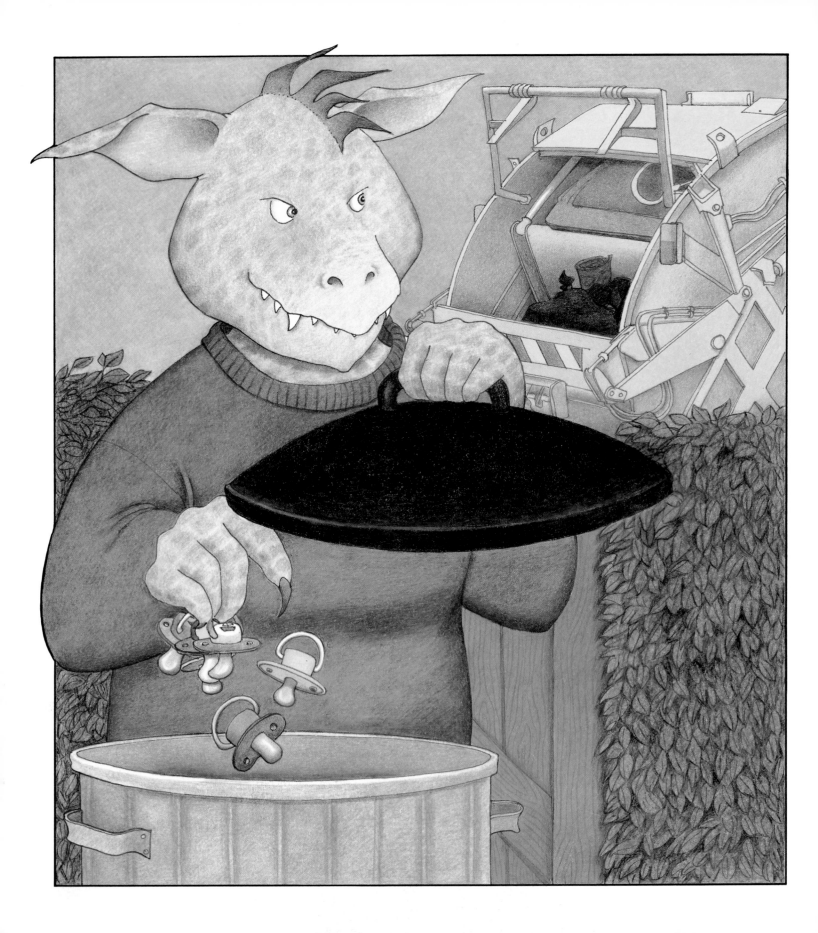

Marlon's mum decided to take drastic action.
She gathered up every single noo-noo she could
find and dumped them all in the dustbin
five minutes before the rubbish truck arrived.
But Marlon had made plans just in case the worst
should happen. He had secret noo-noo supplies
all over the house.

There was a
yellow one down
the side of
the armchair,

a blue one at the back
of the breadbin,

various different types in
his toy ambulance

and his favourite
pink one was lurking
in the toe of his
wellington boot.

His mother and granny were astonished.
They could not think where he kept finding them.
"You'll be teased when you go out to play,"
warned his granny. "A great big monster
like you with a baby's dummy."
Marlon knew about this already. The other
monsters had been teasing him for ages, but he
loved his noo-noos so much that he didn't care.

The other monsters often lay in wait
and jumped out on Marlon as he
passed by with his noo-noo twirling.
"Who's a big baby, then?"
jeered Basher.
"Does the little baby

need his dummy, then?" sneered Alligatina.
"Who's his mummy's little darling?"
cooed Boomps-a-daisy.
Marlon always ignored their taunts.
"You're just jealous," he replied.
"You all wish you'd got one too."

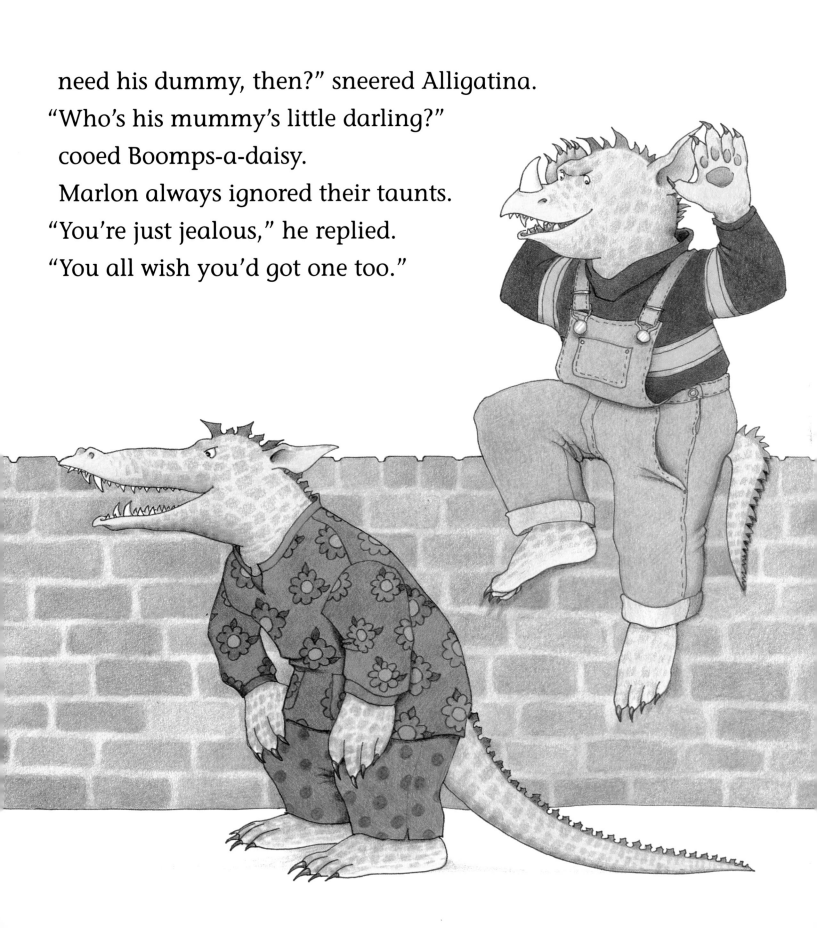

Gradually, the secret supply of noo-noos dwindled. Marlon's mum refused to buy any more and they all began to be lost, or thrown away by Marlon's mum. Finally, there was only one left, the pink one. Marlon kept it with him all the time. Either in his mouth or under his pillow or in the toe of his wellington boot, where no one thought to look.

To his delight, Marlon found one extra noo-noo
that his mum had missed. It was a blue one,
which had fallen down the side of his bed and
been covered up by a sock. He knew his best
pink noo-noo wouldn't last for ever, so he
crept out and planted the blue one
in the garden.

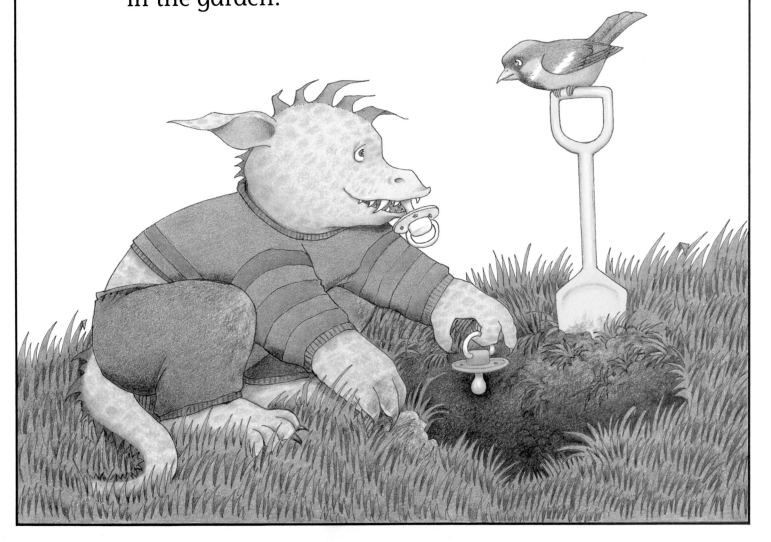

All the other monsters decided
to gang up on Marlon. They
collected lots of different bits of
junk and fixed them all together
until they had made just
what they wanted. It was
a noo-noo snatcher.

Then they waited behind a bush
until Marlon came past with his
pink noo-noo twirling.
"Here he comes," said Alligatina.
"Grab it!" yelled Boomps-a-daisy.
"Now!" said Basher.

With one quick hooking
movement, they caught
the ring of the noo-noo
with the noo-noo snatcher
and pulled!

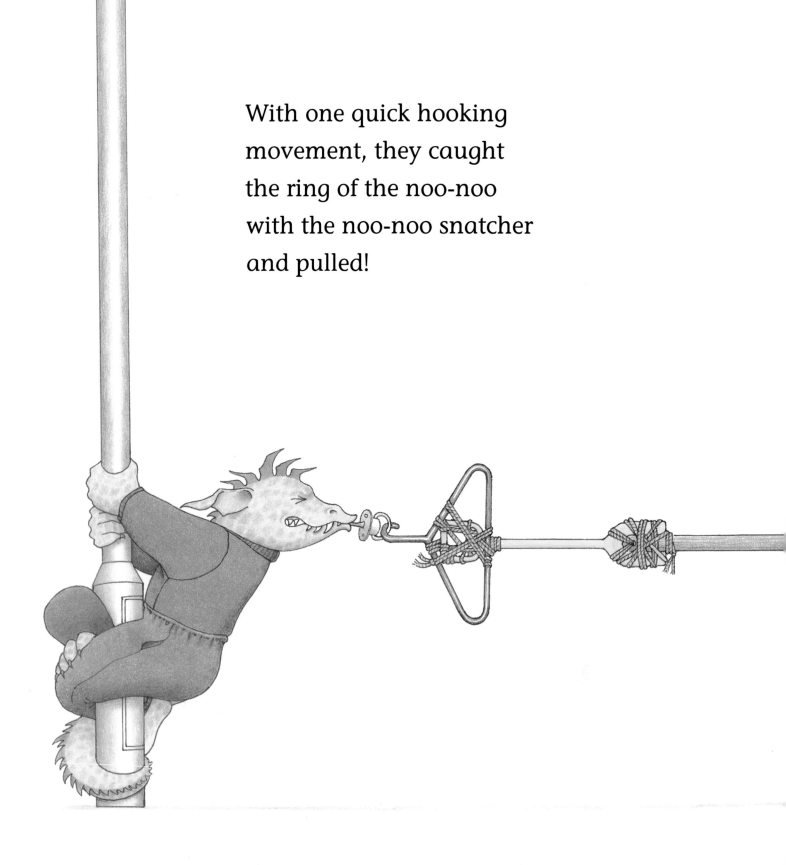

But Marlon clenched his teeth and held on. Monsters have the most powerful jaws in the world. Once they have decided to hang on, that's *it*. Marlon hung on, the monsters hung onto the noo-noo snatcher and there they stayed, both sides pulling with all their monster might.

And there they would *still* be, if Marlon had not decided, just at that very moment, that perhaps he *was* too old to have a noo-noo any more.

So, he let go. And all the other monsters went whizzing off down the road, across the park and into the pond with a mighty splash.

Marlon went home. "I've given up my noo-noo,"
he said. "I sort of threw it into the pond."
"Good gracious me!" exclaimed Marlon's mum,
sitting down suddenly with the shock.
"I told you," said Marlon's granny. "You just
have to be firm."
"Actually," said Marlon, "I've planted one, so I'll
have a noo-noo tree – just in case I change my mind."
"That's nice, dear," said Marlon's mum.

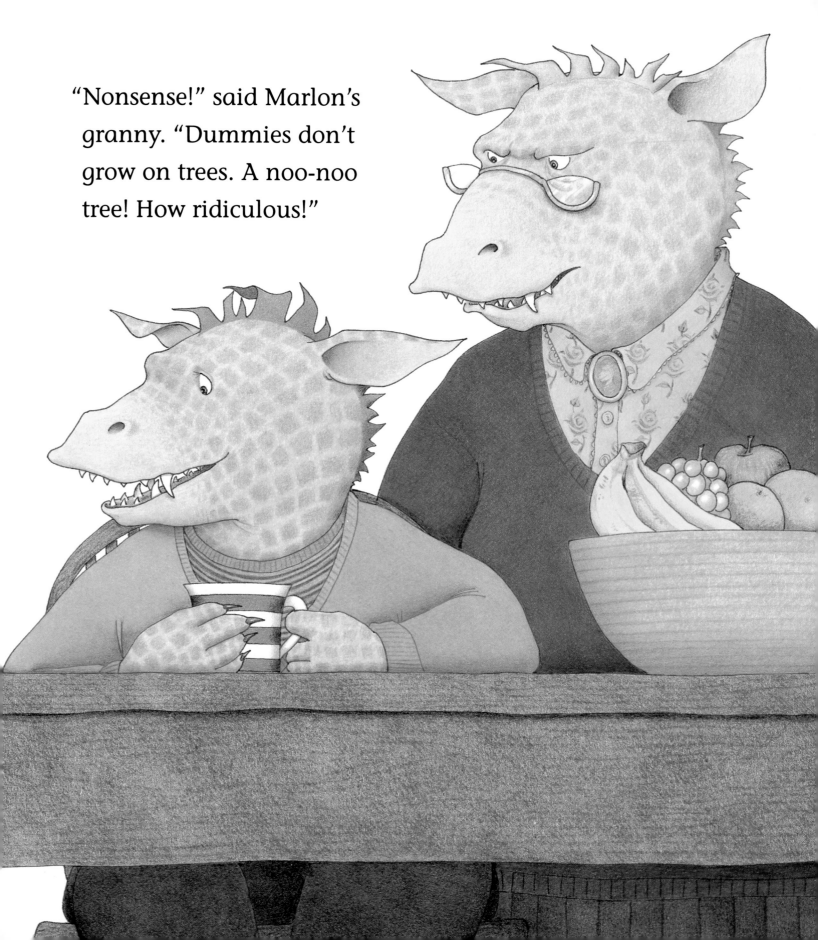

"Nonsense!" said Marlon's granny. "Dummies don't grow on trees. A noo-noo tree! How ridiculous!"